For Fraser

Copyright © 1995 by Ruth Brown
All rights reserved.
CIP Data is available.
Published in the United States 1996 by
Dutton Children's Books,
a division of Penguin Books USA Inc.
375 Hudson Street, New York, New York  10014
Originally published in Great Britain 1995 by
Andersen Press Ltd., London.
Typography by Julia Goodman
Printed in Italy   First American Edition
1 3 5 7 9 10 8 6 4 2
ISBN 0-525-45581-7

# The Ghost of Greyfriar's Bobby

*retold and illustrated by*

## Ruth Brown

DUTTON CHILDREN'S BOOKS ～ *New York*

"How long until we meet Mom and Dad?" Tom moaned.
"I'm hot and thirsty. And I'm sick of sight-seeing."

"We still have a half hour to wait," replied Becky. "You
can get a drink here. Hey, look! It's a fountain for dogs,
too." She read the inscription aloud:

*A tribute to the affectionate fidelity of Greyfriar's Bobby. In 1858, this faithful dog followed the remains of his master to Greyfriar's Churchyard and lingered near the spot until his death in 1872.*

"Let's go into the churchyard, okay, Tom?"

As the children approached the churchyard, the gardener looked up and nodded. "You'll be looking for Bobby, I suppose."

Becky giggled. "We're over a hundred years too late, aren't we?"

"Well, now," said the gardener. "That all depends. If you look hard enough, I think you might see him, lying in the sun in the special place that was his home for so many years.

"Right over there, next to his master, it was. He would sleep there for hours at a time, dreaming of the days before he lived in the churchyard. Bobby always slept in the day-time, you see, because he and old Jock used to work at night when he was a pup.

"Old Jock, Bobby's master, was a cattle herder. He would guard all the beasts that were to be sold at market on the following day.

"In the mornings, after work, Jock and Bobby would visit Mrs. Ramsay's café. She'd always save a special tidbit for Bobby—a bone, a bun, or sometimes even a piece of pie. The other regular customers got to know the little dog as well, and often would welcome him by name.

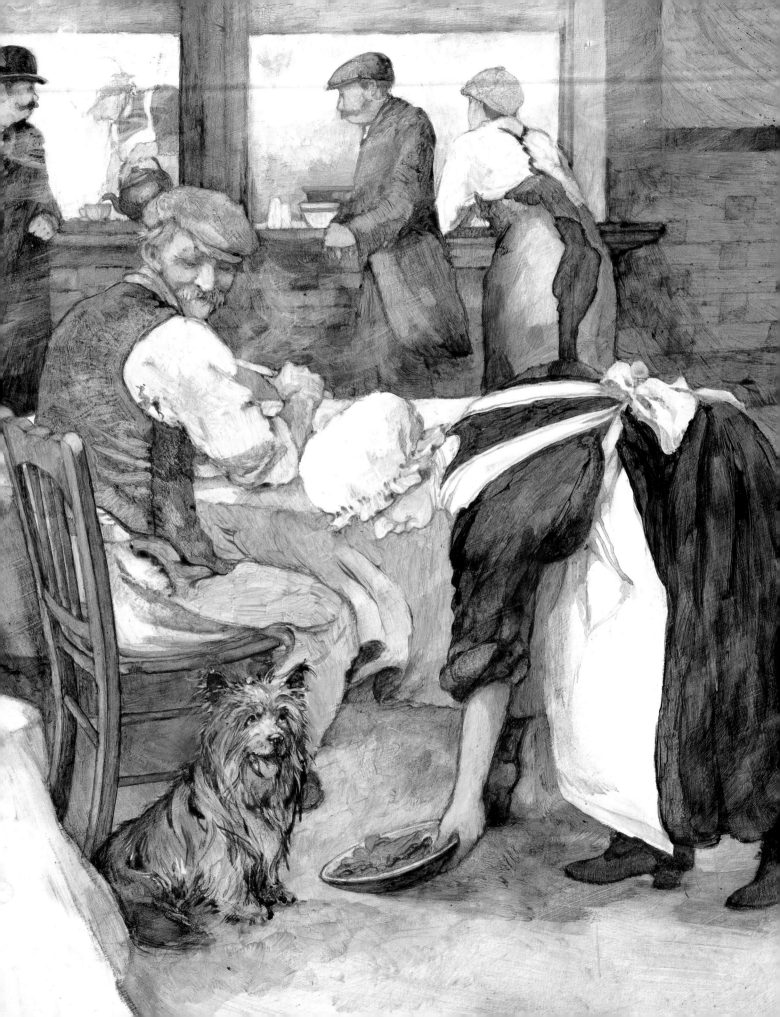

"When they'd get a rare day off, Old Jock and Bobby would walk for miles in the beautiful hills where Jock had lived as a boy.

"But in the winter, they would stay in the city, guarding the cattle night after night. Despite the freezing cold and bitter winds that eventually chased poor Old Jock into a long illness, Bobby stuck close to his master's side.

"One bitter, gray morning, Bobby followed his master for the very last time. It was here that they came, to the churchyard of Greyfriar's, where Old Jock is buried.

"Bobby got as close as he could to Old Jock, and that's where he stayed, but how cold and hungry he was! The granite stone behind him was not much comfort, and his paws were almost frozen to the earth.

"Bobby thought longingly of Mrs. Ramsay's café. If he went there by himself, would she still give him a bone, a bun, or a piece of pie?

"Of course, Mrs. Ramsay remembered the little fellow. And when she found out where he was living, there was food for Bobby every day. The people of the town were so touched by the little dog's loyalty to Jock that they looked after him, and the children always stopped to say hello as they passed.

"Bobby was given a water bowl and his own engraved collar. Best of all, he had official permission to live in the churchyard, right next to Old Jock, and that's where he stayed for fourteen long years."

The gardener paused a moment and leaned on his broom.
"Bobby is buried here, too, of course, very near his beloved
master."

"Wow," said Becky. "What a story!"

"Aye," agreed the gardener. "Bobby never forgot his old
friend, not even for a single day."

"I don't think that we'll ever forget Bobby," said Tom.